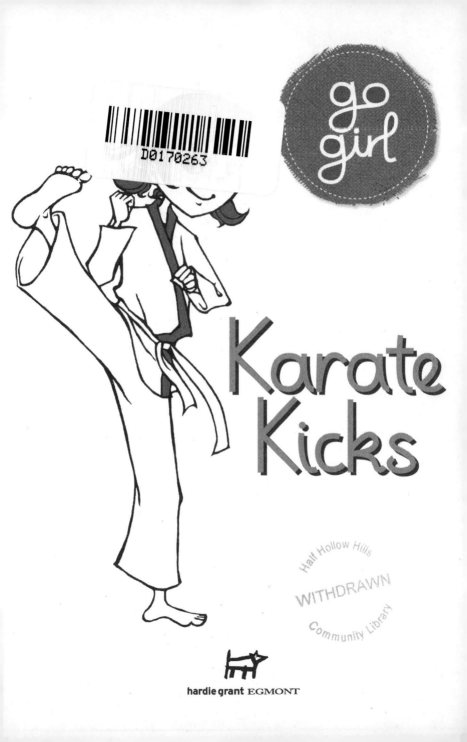

go girl

Karate
Kicks

hardie grant EGMONT

Karate Kicks
first published in 2006
this edition published in 2013 by
Hardie Grant Egmont
Ground Floor, Building 1, 658 Church Street
Richmond, Victoria 3121, Australia
www.hardiegrantegmont.com.au

A CiP record for this title is available from the National Library of Australia

Text copyright © 2006 Chrissie Perry
Illustration and design copyright © 2013 Hardie Grant Egmont

Illustration by Aki Fukuoka
Design by Michelle Mackintosh
Text design and typesetting by Ektavo

Printed in Australia by Griffin Press, an Accredited ISO AS/NZS
14001:2004 Environmental Management System printer.

1 3 5 7 9 10 8 6 4 2

FSC
www.fsc.org
MIX
Paper from
responsible sources
FSC® C009448

The paper this book is printed on is certified against the
Forest Stewardship Council® Standards. Griffin Press holds
FSC chain of custody certification SGS-COC-005088. FSC
promotes environmentally responsible, socially beneficial
and economically viable management of the world's forests

go girl

Karate Kicks

by
Chrissie Perry

Illustrations by
Aki Fukuoka

hardie grant EGMONT

Chapter One

Lola kicked off her school shoes and lay back on the couch. There was a major hole in one of her socks. She poked two toes through the gap, and gave them a wiggle.

As Lola flicked on the TV, the song from *Neighbours* bounced around the lounge room.

Just then, Will kicked his way into the room.

'Hi-ya!' he yelled as he karate-chopped Lola's mermaid statue off the table. Luckily it didn't break. Lola picked it up and tried to squeeze it up with all the other statues and photos on the mantelpiece, but there was no room. She had to put it back on the table. With Will around, that was definitely a worry.

'Sorry about that Lola. Did you make that statue?' Will asked.

'Yes, I made it in art,' Lola said.

'It's really good,' Will offered. 'All your statues are pretty cool.'

Lola smiled. Will could be very nice *sometimes*. But he was also very noisy. She turned up the volume of the TV and settled back into the couch.

'Do you *actually* watch *Neighbours*?' Will asked as he crouched on his knees in the armchair next to the couch. Lola noticed that his nostrils were flared like he was annoyed. One of his eyebrows was raised so high that it looked like it was going to jump off his face.

Lola pulled the sock back over her toes so that Will couldn't see the hole. 'Yeah,' she said quietly.

Will dropped a foot onto the ground and started tapping the floorboards. 'It's a bit lame, don't you think?' he asked. 'Like, as if your neighbours are going to be your best friends.'

Lola bit her lip. Her best friend, Abbey, actually *did* live next door on the third floor of an apartment building next to Lola's house. But somehow, Lola didn't feel like saying anything about that.

'Hey, wanna come outside for a kick?'

Will asked. Lola really just wanted Will to be quiet, so she tried to ignore him and just watch the screen. But in seconds he was back with a football. He handballed it to Lola and it hit her in the chest.

'Outside with the ball, guys,' Lola's mum called out from the kitchen.

Lola sighed, switched off the television, pulled her school shoes back on and went into the backyard with Will.

'Mark this one!' Will called out as he kicked the ball.

Lola put her hands up. She watched — as if in slow motion — as the ball flew through the air towards her. She tried to catch the ball, but it flew straight through her hands and landed on the ground.

Lola picked up the ball and tried to kick it back to Will. But she missed it with her foot. The ball bounced and rolled forwards a couple of metres.

Will flared his nostrils and raised his eyebrows again. It made Lola feel nervous. He raced up to the footy, and handballed it to Lola.

Lola concentrated. She fumbled it a couple of times and then ... dropped it again! She then tried to handball it back. This time it went over Will's head, and into the shed behind him.

'Geez,' Will said from the shed.

Lola heard him rustling around. When he came out, he had dust and cobwebs all over his jumper.

'OK, kick it to me,' Lola urged. She was determined to catch it this time.

'Actually, I think I'll go inside now,' Will said.

'But I was just getting good!' Lola insisted. Will just shrugged and turned to walk into the house.

His eyebrows were raised so high that Lola could have sworn that one of them was missing.

⚡

Chapter Two

A couple of hours later, Lola went up to her room to get ready for bed. She put on her pyjamas. Then she switched on her walkie-talkie.

The set of walkie-talkies had been a present for her last birthday. At first, Lola wasn't excited about them. They lay on her bedroom floor for a week or so, covered by the elephant undies her nanna had given her. But then Abbey had found them and suggested she take one of them up to her bedroom in the flat next door. The girls couldn't believe they actually worked! Since then, Lola and Abbey had spoken to each other almost every night before bed.

Right now, Lola really wanted to talk to her friend.

'Abbey, are you there? Over,' Lola said.

A little crackle flew out of the speaker, followed by Abbey's voice.

'Absolutely here. I'm reading Harry Potter. What are you doing? Over.'

'Just thinking. Are you any good at football? Over,' said Lola.

'Lola you *know* that my relationship with balls isn't good. They are always thwacking me in the head. I find them very rude. Why are you asking me that? Over.'

A big, thudding sound came from Will's bedroom. Lola laid her walkie-talkie on the bed for a moment to listen. Then she picked it up again.

'Can you see what Will's doing from up there? Over,' she asked.

'Hang on, I'm just putting Harry down on the bedside table,' Abbey said. 'OK, I'm up. Will's curtains are open. I can see him. He's wearing something white and he's doing some sort of pose. His arms are kind of up like a kangaroo, and he's got one leg in the air. Now he's kicking his leg out. Over.'

'Don't you think that's kind of weird? Over,' said Lola.

'I think it's karate. Over,' Abbey replied.

'Yeah, but it's *weird*, right?' Lola raised her eyebrows. She wondered if she'd caught the habit from Will.

'Gotta go,' Abbey said. 'Harry Potter is in a sticky situation. Over.'

Lola grinned. Sometimes it was as though Abbey thought Harry Potter was a real boy. Or wizard.

Lola lay back on her bed. Her mum opened the bedroom door and sat next to her like she did every night. It made Lola feel good.

At least *some* things hadn't changed.

Lola was used to having Will and his dad, Rex, at her house *sometimes*. They always used to visit, and sometimes even stay the night. But a week ago, they had moved in for good. Having Will around all the time was *very* different.

'How are you going with Will, sweetie?' her mum asked.

It sure is different!

Lola didn't know what to say.

Her mum looked so happy. She really seemed to love Rex. And Lola liked Rex and Will too. It was just that her life was so different with them here. It seemed so *busy* all the time compared with how it used to be. Sometimes it felt like Will and Rex had lived here forever, and *she* was the new one.

'Will's OK,' Lola said softly. Another thump came from Will's bedroom.

'Even though he can be *very* loud!' said Lola's mum.

'And fidgety,' Lola added.

Her mum gave her a funny smile and Lola giggled. Then her mum started laughing. Another big thump came from Will's bedroom and they both cracked up. And then every time they heard another thud, it set them off again.

'I guess we'll get used to it,' Lola giggled.

Her mum hugged her tight. 'I'm sure we will,' her mum said.

Chapter Three

'Hey Lola, can you hop in the car, please?' asked Lola's mum. 'I have to take Will to karate.'

'Mum, I'm in the middle of my homework,' Lola said.

'It won't take long, sweetie. We can have a hot chocolate while he's at class.'

Lola put her pencils back in the pencil case as Will came tumbling into the room.

He was dressed all in white, with big pants, a loose jacket and a white belt tied around the middle.

Will hopped unsteadily on one foot. His other leg rose into the air. Lola grabbed her mermaid statue and held it safely in her hands out of his way.

'Yo, I'm the Karate Kid! Look at this,' Will exclaimed. He squatted down with his knees, bent his elbows and raised his hands together in the air. His face went red with concentration. It looked very funny against the whiteness of his clothes.

Lola giggled.

'Ha, you may laugh at my Horse Stance,' Will said, 'but one day, you will realise my ultimate power and you shall laugh no more!'

Lola bit her lip to stop herself from laughing out loud. 'Will, how many karate classes have you done so far?' Lola asked.

'This will be my second lesson, Grass-hopper,' said Will.

Lola snuck a little eye-roll at her mum, and her mum winked back.

'Jump into the car, grasshoppers,' her mum joked.

⚡

Lola watched as the karate students entered the hall. At the doorway, each of them dropped their heads and bowed. Even Will did it.

Lola nudged her mum. 'Why do they do that?' she asked.

'I'm not sure,' her mum replied.

Lola was a bit surprised to see that there were girls in the karate class. All of the kids had the same white uniform, with the white belt tied around it. Only the teacher had a black belt. Lola knew that meant he was really, really good at karate. But he didn't look like a fighter. He had a great big smile and twinkly eyes.

The instructor spoke to Lola. 'Welcome to our class,' he said. 'Next time you enter or exit through that door, you should bow. It's to show respect for each other, and the art of karate.'

Lola nodded. She liked that idea.

The instructor looked over at Will and his friend Patrick, and shook his head. The boys were play fighting, and making a lot of noise.

The instructor walked over to them. 'Boys, you're reminding me of a pair of chihuahuas,' he said. His grin was wide and his voice was soft. But the boys still stopped fighting to listen.

'The chihuahua is a small dog with a loud bark,' he said. 'The aim of karate is to give you skill and confidence with your bodies. But your mind is your best tool.

Your mind should tell you when to bark, and when to stay quiet. And, with practice, you will have great skill in both your mind and your body, and you will no longer feel the need to act like the chihuahua. Do you understand, boys?'

Will and Patrick nodded and settled down.

'Now, do you remember how to do the Attention Stance?'

All the karate students stood very straight with their hands at their sides. Lola thought they looked graceful. Even Will looked calm and still for a change.

'Do you want to get a hot chocolate now?' Lola's mum whispered.

Lola nodded, and they tiptoed out.

Without thinking, Lola bowed her head
a little as she left the hall.

As they sat in a cafe and ordered drinks, Lola kept thinking about the karate class.

There was something about the teacher and the uniforms that made her much more interested than she thought she would be. As she took a sip of her hot chocolate, she thought about how the teacher had told the students to keep their weight evenly on both feet and to stand tall. And even though she was sitting down, Lola found that she was trying to follow his instructions.

'Mum, do you think it's too late for me to join the karate class?' Lola asked.

Her mum smiled. 'Let me check that

out for you. I'm sure Will would love you to go with him,' she said.

Lola hadn't imagined how Will might feel about her joining the class.

But she was going to find out.

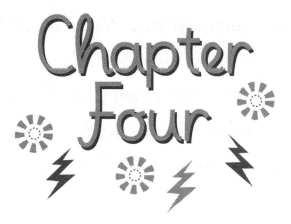

Chapter Four

'Lola, come over to my place for a sleep-over. We can make up a concert. Over,' Abbey's voice came through the walkie-talkie. 'And bring the red skirt, a pair of your mum's high heels, and the green clip-on earrings. Oh, and some CDs. Over.'

'Do you want me to bring the kitchen sink? Over,' Lola joked.

'Nah. But maybe some of those yummy muesli bars. The ones with the chocolate chips. Over,' Abbey said.

Lola asked her mum if it was OK to stay over at Abbey's, and then collected all the things she needed. Her hands were full as she went into the kitchen to get the muesli bars. She put the walkie-talkie down on a ledge in the pantry as she popped the bars in her pocket. Then she staggered over to Abbey's.

Lola loved making up concerts with Abbey. Abbey's bed was like a bouncy stage. Sometimes they would sing together without music. Other times, when Abbey's brother went out, they would borrow his

CD player, and sing along with their favourite songs.

Tonight Abbey's brother was home, so they had to go without the music. Lola didn't care. It was fun anyway. First, they got all dressed up. Abbey put on Lola's red skirt and the old clip-on earrings, and Lola put on Abbey's big, green feather boa over her favourite pyjamas and a tiara. Then, Abbey snuck into her mum's room, and came back with all sorts of make-up.

Abbey put eye shadow on Lola with a cotton bud. It felt like butterflies moving across her eyelids. Then Lola did the same for Abbey. They each applied their own lipstick. Then, they were ready.

Abbey always hogged the toy microphone, so Lola just sang into a small teddy.

It was pretty funny. Abbey's singing
voice was terrible, but she made up for
it with her dance moves. In fact, Abbey

danced so much that Lola was *moved* right off the stage! She landed next to Abbey's walkie-talkie.

'Use *that* as a microphone,' Abbey yelled, doing a special move that involved putting her head down, then flicking her hair back wildly.

Lola grinned. She picked up the walkie-talkie, and climbed back on the bed. She turned it on, and began singing along with Abbey. Then she heard something.

'Sshhhh,' Lola said. There were voices coming from the other receiver.

'Listen, it's Will talking to his dad. I must have left my walkie-talkie on in the pantry. I just heard my name!'

Abbey stopped dancing and sat on the bed. Lola sat next to her and held the walkie-talkie between them so they could both hear.

'But Dad, it's not fair!' Will was saying. 'Patrick is in the karate class with me. It would just be *so* embarrassing …'

'Why would it be embarrassing, Will? I think it would be good for you two to do something together.'

'All right then, I'll find something we can do together. But you should see how hopeless she is at footy, dad. I mean, she's *really* unco-ordinated. She can't even mark the ball from …' Will's voice trailed off. Then it started up again.

'… Dad, I just want to do karate on my own,' Will moaned.

'Come on Will, stop being silly,' said Rex.

'I'm NOT being silly,' Will yelled. 'I hate it here. I want to go home!'

Chapter Five

There was a long silence and Abbey and Lola pushed their ears right up next to the walkie-talkie. Rex's voice was really soft when he spoke again. Lola couldn't quite make out what he'd said. But it was very easy to hear Will's reply.

'It's not *my* home, Dad! It's Lola's home. Look, Dad, there's nothing of ours here! There's not even any room for any of our stuff.' Will sounded really upset.

Lola held her breath.

For the first time, she saw the house through Will's eyes. She knew exactly what was on the mantelpiece. There were photos of Lola alone and photos of Lola with her mum. There were statues and plates she'd made in art. And there was hardly a gap anywhere.

Poor Will!

Lola finally let the breath out, trying to make it silent. But it came out like a long sigh. She imagined what it would be like if she and her mum had moved into Rex's house, with all of Will's things around. Abbey would have hated it too.

There was a really loud squeaking noise as the pantry door opened. Lola and Abbey dropped the walkie-talkie that had been pressed right up next to their ears.

'I'll just finish tidying up here, and then let's go kick the footy together in the park. Just you and me. OK, matey?' Rex's voice sounded really close, like he was in the pantry. 'Oh, look – Lola left her walkie-talkie on in the pantry,' he said.

Just then, Abbey's walkie-talkie stopped crackling. Rex must have turned Lola's off.

'Will is *so* mean,' Abbey said. 'Why should he care if you do the karate class with him?'

Lola shook her head. In a way, she agreed with Abbey. It *was* a bit mean of Will to try to exclude her from karate. But in another way, she understood how he was feeling. Lola suddenly didn't feel like playing dress-ups anymore. She put down the walkie-talkie and wiped off her make-up.

'I think I'll pull out of the karate class, Abbey,' Lola said.

'You can't do that!' Abbey replied. 'If you want to do karate, you can't let Will stop you. He's going to be around all the time now, Lola. If you let him stop you doing things, who knows where it will end?'

Lola closed her eyes and lay back on Abbey's bed. It was pretty hard to decide what to do about karate. It seemed like everyone was right in their own way.

Abbey was right about not letting Will stop her from doing stuff. And Will had a point about wanting to keep some things the same, after there had been so many changes lately.

Lola opened her eyes and sat up suddenly. She had an idea. Maybe she could make things better for Will *and* join the karate class?

It was worth a try.

Chapter Six

'Rex, where are all of Will's things?' Lola asked. It was a Monday afternoon so Will was at cricket training, and Lola's mum was still at work. Lola was getting used to having afternoon tea just with Rex.

Rex opened the oven, and waved a tea towel around. 'Anzac biscuits!' he said. 'Careful, Lola, they're ... ouch!'

'Hot?' Lola offered.

Rex ran his finger under the kitchen tap. 'Yeah, hot,' he agreed, flicking a biscuit across the bench.

Lola caught the biscuit and took a bite. 'Yummo,' she said.

Rex smiled. 'Now, what did you ask?' he said.

Lola nearly reminded him that he shouldn't talk with his mouth full. 'I just wondered if Will had some things I could put around the house? You know, to make him feel a bit more at home.'

Rex draped the tea towel over his shoulder and leaned on the bench. He looked at Lola closely.

For a second, she was worried he was

going to ask where she got the idea from. She didn't fancy telling him that she'd overheard their argument.

'Look under his bed,' Rex said. 'I think there's a box of photos and trophies and stuff there.'

'OK,' said Lola. 'Can I take another Anzac bickie?'

Rex smiled, and passed her three more biscuits. 'Don't tell your mum, though,' he said with a wink.

⚡

Lola pulled the box out from under Will's bed. On the top, there was a baby photo of him all dressed up like a pixie. Will's hair had been really curly. It was popping out of a high green hat.

Lola thought about her favourite baby photo. It was of her when she was a chubby baby. Her mum had dressed her up as an angel, with wings and everything. Will's photo could go up next to that. They would look really cute together!

Underneath the pixie photo in Will's box there was a whole heap of trophies. Lola was a little bit shocked. She only had one trophy, and that was just for being part of a netball team. Will's trophies all had things like 'Best and Fairest' engraved on them.

Lola dragged the box downstairs. She took some of her own pictures and statues down. Then she put Will's stuff all around the lounge room.

When she had finished, she stared up at the mantelpiece. It had been quite hard to decide what to take down.

Will is going to love this!

Everything up there had its own story. Like the mug she'd painted for Mother's Day. And the photo of her going down a slide, with her hair blowing behind her. Lola actually remembered that moment. It was the first time she'd gone down the big slide in the park by herself. She had felt so brave.

But Lola didn't mind taking her special things down. She liked having her stuff around the house. And she hoped that Will would feel the same way.

It was five o'clock when she finished. Lola sat on the couch and looked around. The lounge room seemed really different.

She heard Will banging through the

front door, and throwing his schoolbag down in the hallway.

'I'm STARVING!' he called out. 'What's that smell, Dad? Did you make …'

Will raced into the lounge room and right through to the kitchen. It seemed as though he hadn't noticed anything.

But then, he turned around sharply and came back into the lounge with Rex right behind him.

As Will looked around, his face broke into a huge grin.

'Dad, did you …?' he began.

Rex handed Will an Anzac biscuit.

'Nup, Lola did it all,' he said softly.

For a minute, Will just stood there,

munching on his biscuit. Finally, he looked at Lola.

'If you want to join the karate class I'd better teach you some of the moves,' he said. 'You're already three classes behind the others.'

Lola smiled and got up from the couch and stood beside Will.

He balanced a biscuit on his head.

'So, this is how you do the Attention Stance,' he said.

Will was a really good teacher. Over the next few days he gave Lola karate lessons after school. They would push the furniture to the side of the lounge room so there was more space to practise in.

'OK, I think you have the Attention Stance nailed, Grasshopper,' he said on the third afternoon.

Lola bowed to him.

'Why, thank you for your noble lesson, Grasshopper Will,' she said.

Will laughed. He put his head on the couch, flipped his legs up in the air and waggled them around wildly.

For a moment, as he was upside down, he kind of looked like a grasshopper. Lola cracked up laughing, but soon she was on the armchair next to him and copying his leg movements.

'You look funny in that baby photo,' Will said.

'Of course it looks funny when you're upside down. *Your* baby photo looks funny from here too,' Lola said.

'Nup, you look funny anyway,' Will replied.

Lola giggled. The blood was rushing to her head and it began to feel weird. She sat upright.

'It's actually kind of nice having your photos up there too,' she said. 'At Abbey's place there are heaps of photos of her with her brothers. Sometimes I used to look at them and wish ...' Lola's voice trailed off.

Will flung his legs down to the floor and stared at the photos.

'Me too,' he said. 'Being an only child is a bit boring sometimes, isn't it?'

Lola nodded.

'I used to wonder what it would be like if there were more kids in my family,' he continued. 'Like, a little brother to do karate with would be perfect!' he teased.

Lola narrowed her eyes and shook her head at Will.

'I actually wanted a *sister* or two, myself,' she joked.

Will jumped up and started chasing Lola around the lounge room. It was hard to run and laugh at the same time. But she was still quicker than Will and eventually he gave up.

They moved all the furniture back from the sides of the room together. Lola was puffing and panting when she looked at the clock.

'Excellent!' she said, 'We're just in time for *Neighbours*.'

Will rolled his eyes. 'I'm outta here,' he said, racing around the sofa and out of the lounge room. Lola waited for the sound of his footsteps up the stairs. But his footsteps seemed to stop suddenly.

From where she was sitting, Lola could just see a shadow of someone in the hall-way. It looked like the person had their head turned towards the television. And the person looked suspiciously like Will.

Chapter Eight

Lola was excited about her first karate class. Her mum had even bought her a karate uniform with a pink collar and a matching head band.

She felt really special in the uniform. It was loose, and easy to move and kick in. It was as though just putting it on made Lola a real karate student. She couldn't wait to try out the Attention Stance in a real class, with the proper karate clothes.

They were the first ones to turn up at the hall. Lola remembered to bow her head at the door.

Then the instructor arrived, chatting with a group of kids.

'Come and I'll show you how to warm up,' Will said. They took off their shoes and stood on the mat. As they stretched, Patrick squeezed in between Lola and Will.

'Geez mate, did they make you bring your unco sister in the end? That sucks! And what's with her pink, girly uniform?' Patrick was kind of whispering. But it was a loud, hoarse whisper, as though he really *wanted* Lola to hear.

Lola kept her head down, but turned it to one side so she could see Will. She wished he would say something to Patrick. She wished he would tell Patrick to stop talking about her. But all Will did was look down at his feet.

Lola felt as though her heart had stopped. Suddenly, her karate costume felt like a silly dress-up. She *was* unco. She had never won a trophy like Will. Of course she would be hopeless at karate.

But there was one thing that bothered her even more than the thought that she might be hopeless at karate. It was that Will didn't even stick up for her.

Lola had really enjoyed practising karate

with Will. She felt like she'd finally got to know him. But now it just felt as though he was a stranger. As though all the time they had spent together practising karate didn't mean anything!

I feel so silly!

Lola moved into the front row. She wished the mat was bigger, so she could be further away from Will and Patrick.

Lola concentrated really hard once the class started and followed all the moves the instructor called out. As they were doing the Horse Stance, the instructor walked around the class commenting on their stances.

'You are doing *very* well for your first lesson,' he said to Lola. 'Did someone help you?'

Lola looked over her shoulder at Will.

'Not really,' she fibbed. She didn't feel like giving Will any credit at the moment. As far as Lola was concerned, she was on her own in this class. And she certainly

wouldn't be asking for any more help from him!

The rest of the class went well. Lola was surprised, but it seemed that feeling angry made her quite strong.

The instructor put them in pairs. One student had to try to push the other one over, and the other had to use a special sideways move to avoid them. Lola teamed up with Lisa.

'I really like your pink uniform, Lola,' Lisa said before they started the exercise. That made Lola feel better. It also made her feel better that Lisa had been doing karate for years, but Lola managed to keep up with her quite well. She was so involved that she almost forgot about Will and Patrick. Almost.

'That was great guys,' the instructor said at the end of the lesson. 'Next Saturday we are going to have a special training session. I will divide you into teams on the day, and we'll have a competition in the park outside the hall.'

A few kids cheered. They had obviously been looking forward to the special training session. Lola was keen too. It sounded cool. But she hoped she wouldn't be on the same team as Will and Patrick.

⚡

Chapter Nine

Lola didn't feel like speaking on the way home from the class. She sat right on the edge of the back seat. Will sat on the other side. Both of them wound down their windows.

'So, how did it go?' asked her mum.

'Fine,' Will said into the wind.

'Yeah, fine,' Lola repeated.

'I like the way you have to bow before

you enter the hall,' said Lola's mum. 'It's a great way of remembering to have respect for each other, don't you think?'

This time, neither of them answered. Lola snuck a look at Will. He avoided her eyes but Lola could tell he felt guilty. And so he should! Lola tried to move even further away from him. The rest of the trip was completely silent.

I'm never talking to Will again!

When they got home, Lola watched *Neighbours* and Will went to his room.

At dinner, only their parents were talking.

'You guys are very quiet. You must be exhausted. It's normally a zoo around here,' Rex said. He had a worried look on his face. Lola noticed that her mum had the same expression.

'So, what's on this weekend?' Lola's mum asked. Will and Lola both shrugged.

'Well, you have Patrick coming to stay tomorrow night, Will,' Rex said brightly.

Lola put down her fork. Even though

spaghetti bolognaise was her favourite, she couldn't eat another bite. It was bad enough sharing her house with Will at the moment. She couldn't bear to share it with Patrick as well.

'Can I stay at Abbey's place tomorrow night, mum?' Lola asked.

Her mum frowned. 'I guess so, sweetie,' she said sadly.

The next day Abbey came to Lola's house to pick her up for the sleep-over. She had a long list of things she wanted Lola to bring. When Abbey saw the biscuits Rex had made, her list grew even longer!

After she had packed some bickies, Lola fished around in her drawers for her best pyjamas.

Abbey sat on the bed. 'What time is Dorkas coming over?' she asked.

Lola had told Abbey all about Patrick and the first karate class. Ever since then, Abbey had called Patrick 'Dorkas'. The way Abbey said it, in a low voice, always made Lola laugh.

'Dorkas should be here in about half an hour,' Lola replied, finally finding the yellow pyjamas with grey elephants on them under her bed. Lola put them in her backpack and sat on the bed with Abbey.

'So I think that's everything,' she said.

'Not quite,' said Abbey.

Lola rolled her eyes and fell back on the bed. 'All right, slave driver,' she joked, 'what else do you want me to do?'

Abbey clasped her hands together and narrowed her eyes. 'I want you to plant your walkie-talkie in Will's room,' she whispered.

Lola screwed up her nose. 'Why?' she asked.

Abbey walked to the window, and pointed up at her room. 'You know, I can see into Will's bedroom very clearly from up there,' she said.

'I know,' said Lola. 'So?'

'So, we have the picture, but not the sound. Don't you want to hear what the boys talk about?'

'Not really,' said Lola.

'Yes you do!' Abbey insisted. 'It would be fun. We might even get to hear their secrets!'

I can't spy on Will... or can I?

Lola thought about it for a moment.

It wasn't very nice to spy on someone. But then again, Will hadn't been very nice to her lately. He hadn't even stuck up for her at karate. Maybe he deserved to be spied on?

'I reckon we'd be able to hear them if we put the walkie-talkie under Will's bed,' Lola suggested.

⚡

Chapter Ten

'No, go left. Push the X button. Now try to go through that door.'

Patrick's voice came through over the walkie-talkie, together with zooming and crashing noises from the computer game they were playing.

Abbey lay on the bed, sharing out the biscuits.

'Hey, you've got an extra one!' Lola

complained. Abbey broke the biscuit in half and handed one of the pieces to Lola.

'How long can they play that game for?' Abbey asked.

'Well, if they had enough food and water, I reckon about twenty years!' Lola laughed.

Abbey turned down the volume on the walkie-talkie. The crashing noises faded.

Then she got up from the bed, and stared out the window. Abbey had a funny look in her eyes.

'What?' Lola demanded.

'Don't you think Patrick looks a bit like the guy from X-Press?' Abbey asked.

'Abbey!' Lola exclaimed. 'He's a dorkas,

remember? You gave him that name yourself!'

Abbey grinned. 'That was before I saw him,' she said softly.

Lola shook her head, and turned up the volume of the walkie-talkie. This time there was no crash-bashing from the game.

'Hey, they're actually talking,' Lola said. Lola and Abbey stood side by side at the window, with the walkie-talkie between them.

'The training session is going to be so cool,' Patrick said. 'So long as your unco sister isn't on our team, I think we'll win.'

'She's not really my sister,' Will said.

Lola held her breath. She knew that she wasn't really Will's sister. But the way he said it was as though he was embarrassed by her. She was nervous about what he would say next.

Suddenly, putting Lola's walkie-talkie under Will's bed seemed like a very bad idea.

Abbey seemed to sense Lola's nerves. She put her arms around Lola's shoulder. It seemed like forever until Will spoke again.

'And she's actually not that unco-ordinated,' he said.

Lola let the breath out.

'You were the one that told me Lola was unco,' Patrick said.

'Yeah, but that was ages ago,' Will replied. 'And I just thought that because she was hopeless at footy. She's actually pretty good at karate.'

Then Patrick spoke again. 'Did you see how Lola was blocking Lisa? And Lisa's been doing karate for ages,' Patrick said.

Will laughed. 'Yeah, I reckon Lisa got

Lola is actually really good at karate!

a bit of a shock,' he said. 'You know, Lola learned the hand blocking really quickly,' Will continued. 'It took me ages to get it right. I can usually block Mario now. And I can trip him about half the time. The only one in the class I've never beaten is Big Ben. He's *so* strong, that guy.'

'Yeah, let's face it Will. You're just like an insect to Big Ben. Like a little, annoying fly.' Patrick started making buzzing noises, and soon the boys were play fighting again.

'Will finally stood up for you, Lola,' Abbey said. Lola noticed that Abbey was watching all of Patrick's moves through the window.

'Yeah, I guess he did, kind of,' she began. 'But I don't know if I really trust him anymore. He should have stood up for me in the class. Or at least, he should have said sorry afterwards.'

Abbey sighed. 'You're right, Lola. But you know it's never perfect living with boys.'

'What do you mean?' asked Lola.

Abbey grinned. 'I'll show you what I

mean. Listen to this.' Abbey opened her bedroom door.

'Robert, can I borrow your CD player?' she yelled down the hallway. Robert's voice instantly boomed back.

'You touch my CD player, and I'll break you in half!'

Abbey came back into her room and closed the door. 'See?' she said.

Lola smiled. 'Yeah, I see,' she said. 'I know Will and I will have fights. But I just want to know I can trust him, deep down. Robert might be a pain, but I remember when he told Tom off for picking on you at school ...'

Lola stopped talking.

Abbey wasn't listening. She was still looking out the window.

'Maybe I'll come and watch the training session,' Abbey said dreamily.

Lola giggled into her pillow. 'Your sudden interest in karate doesn't have anything to do with Patrick, does it?' she asked.

'What? Dorkas? Of course not,' Abbey said.

Chapter Eleven

'The team lists are up on the noticeboard,' said the instructor. 'Have a look at who you are with and then we'll start the competition. And don't forget that we'll be having a barbecue afterwards, thanks to all the parents who provided the food!'

Lola looked over to the side of the hall. Rex and her mum were sitting with all the other parents. Abbey was sitting on the bench beside them. Lola noticed that she was wearing her favourite jeans and a new T-shirt.

There was a rush as everyone went to look at the list. Lola craned her neck, looking for her name.

Lola gasped. She hadn't expected the teams to be divided this way. When she had thought about the training session, she'd always thought that Will and Patrick would be on the same team.

Oh no! Will is on the other team!

Sometimes she'd thought she'd be on the opposite team to them, and sometimes she'd thought she would be on the same team. But the idea of her and Patrick being against Will hadn't even crossed her mind.

'OK, teams. Outside now,' said the instructor. 'Team B will be the first attackers. Try to make a surprise attack on a member of Team A. Team A, your job is to deal with the surprise attack, using any of the moves we've learned in class. Remember, there is to be no violence and no hard contact. The attackers will only try to push, and the defenders will try to stop them. Are we clear?'

Everyone nodded. Patrick and Lola walked outside with the rest of their team.

'Hey, who's your friend?' Patrick asked, pointing to Abbey. Lola noticed that he was spiking up his hair with his fingers.

'I'll tell you later,' Lola said. 'Right now, we should be preparing for –'

Just that second, Lisa jumped out of the bushes and pushed Patrick. He was totally unprepared and went down quickly.

'Hey, I wasn't ready!' he complained.

But Lola wasn't listening.

I need to be ready for a surprise attack!

She got ready for an attack. She pivoted, using the Horse Stance to keep her steady.

Suddenly, Big Ben jumped out from behind a tree. His hands were coming towards her. But Lola was ready.

Hi-ya!

She grabbed him by the arm, and put her foot behind his leg.

She was winning!

Big Ben was going down.

But the next thing she knew, Lola had lost her balance. Big Ben was down, but Lola had tripped over him. She lunged forward. Her foot hit a tree stump. Her ankle twisted painfully.

Lola sat by the stump, holding her ankle. She squeezed her eyes closed, trying not to cry. Everyone stopped, and rushed over to her.

Lola heard Big Ben apologising.

Then she heard Will's voice. 'Go and get an ice-pack, Patrick. And some bandages. Run!'

Will crouched beside Lola. 'Are you all right?' he asked. His voice was full of concern.

The instructor ran over to them. He examined Lola's ankle. 'It's OK, Will,' he said. 'It's just a bad sprain. I'll take care of Lola. You go back to the competition.'

Will shook his head. 'I want to stay here,' he said. 'With my ... well she is kind of my ... sister,' he said.

Lola looked at Will and attempted a smile.

Even though her ankle hurt pretty badly, part of her was happy. She knew now that she could trust Will when it really counted.

Chapter Twelve

Afterwards, at the barbecue, Lola sat with her bandaged ankle up on a chair. Will, Patrick and Abbey had each brought a sausage over for her.

Now they were all coming towards her with cake. Patrick and Abbey were walking together. Lola grinned as Patrick ran his fingers through his hair ... again!

'How's the hero?' Rex asked, sitting beside her.

Lola laughed. 'What do you mean?' she asked.

Rex leant in towards her. 'Everyone's talking about how you tripped Big Ben!' he said. 'Even the instructor can't believe it.'

When they got home that night, Lola limped from the car, and just about fell onto the couch. She was full of sausages and cake. And she was completely exhausted.

Her eyelids grew heavy. She closed her eyes, and began drifting off to sleep.

Then she felt a tap on her shoulder.

'Hey, it's six-thirty,' Will said. 'Isn't it time for your lame show?' He put his head on the armchair, and did the grasshopper leg waggle.

Lola switched on the TV.

The *Neighbours* song bounced around the room. Lola choked back a laugh. Will may have been upside down, but he was watching with her.

Lola smiled. Her team had lost the competition. And her ankle was really throbbing – but somehow, that didn't matter.

Lola still felt like a winner.